Edmund Gosse

In Russet & Silver

Edmund Gosse

In Russet & Silver

ISBN/EAN: 9783337165192

Printed in Europe, USA, Canada, Australia, Japan

Cover: Foto ©Andreas Hilbeck / pixelio.de

More available books at **www.hansebooks.com**

In Russet & Silver

In Russet & Silver

By

Edmund Gosse

Chicago
Stone & Kimball
MDCCCXCIV

Contents

Contents

POEMS OF EXPERIENCE

LYRICS

Contents

Contents

DEDICATION

TO

TUSITALA IN VAILIMA

1

Cleareſt voice in Britain's chorus,
      Tuſitala !
Years ago, years four and twenty,
Grey the cloudland drifted o'er us,
When theſe ears firſt heard you talking,
When theſe eyes firſt ſaw you ſmiling.

Years of famine, years of plenty,
Years of beckoning and beguiling,
Years of yielding, ſhifting, baulking, —
When the good ſhip " Clanſman" bore us
Round the ſpits of Tobermory,
Glens of Voulin like a viſion,

Dedication

Crags of Knoidart, huge and hoary, —
We had laughed in light derifion,
Had they told us, told the daring
                                    Tufitala,
What the years' pale hands were bearing, —
Years in ftately, dim divifion.

II

Now the fkies are pure above you,
                                    Tufitala;
Feather'd trees bow down to love you;
Perfum'd winds from fhining waters
Stir the fanguine-leav'd hibifcus   ·
That your kingdom's dufk-ey'd daughters
Weave about their fhining treffes;
Dew-fed guavas drop their vifcous
Honey at the fun's careffes,
Where eternal fummer bleffes
Your ethereal mufky highlands; —
Ah! but does your heart remember,
                                    Tufitala,
Weftward in our Scotch September,
Blue againft the pale fun's ember, —

Dedication

That low rim of faint long iflands,
Barren granite-fnouted neffes,
Plunging in the dull'd Atlantic,
Where beyond Tiree one gueffes
At the full tide, loud and frantic?

III

By ftrange pathways God hath brought you,
                                  Tufitala,
In ftrange webs of fortune caught you,
Led you by ftrange moods and meafures
To this paradife of pleafures!
And the body-guard that fought you
To conduct you home to glory, —
Dark the oriflammes they carried,
In the mift their cohort tarried, —
They were Languor, Pain, and Sorrow,
                                  Tufitala!
Scarcely we endured their ftory
Trailing on from morn to morrow,
Such the devious road they led you,
Such the error, fuch the vaftnefs,

Dedication

Such the cloud that overſpread you,
Under exile bow'd and baniſh'd,
Loſt, like Moſes in the faſtneſs,
Till we almoſt deem'd you vaniſh'd.

IV

Vaniſh'd? ay, that's ſtill the trouble.
Tuſitala!
Though your tropic iſle rejoices,
'T is to us an Iſle of Voices
Hollow like the elfin double
Cry of diſembodied echoes,
Or an owlet's wicked laughter,
Or the cold and horned gecko's
Croaking from a ruined rafter, —
Voices theſe of things exiſting,
Yet inceſſantly reſiſting
Eyes and hands that follow after ;
You are circled, as by magic,
In a ſurf-built palmy bubble,
Tuſitala ;
Fate hath choſen, but the choice is
Half deleɛtable, half tragic,

Dedication

For we hear you speak, like Moses,
And we greet you back, enchanted,
But reply's no sooner granted,
Than the rifted cloud-land closes.

September, 1894.

In Russet & Silver

Life, that, when youth was hot and bold,
Leaped up in scarlet and in gold,
Now walks, by graver hopes possessed,
In russet and in silver dressed.

IN RUSSET AND SILVER

THIS body, that was warm of old,
And supple, grows constrained and cold ;
These hands are drawn and dry, these eyes
Less eager as they grow more wise.

The sunlight where I used to lie
And bathe as in a pool of sky,
Is now too violent and bold,
And makes my nerves ache.   I grow old.

When I was young, and did not know
The blessedness of being so,
Stray glances set me on the rack,
And sent strange shivers down my back.

But now those very glances seem
To come from phantoms in a dream ;
The unknown eyes that flashed, divine,
Must now be middle-aged, like mine.

In Russet and Silver

And tho' I'm blithe and boisterous yet,
With all my cronies round me set,
There enters one who's really young,
And I grow grey.   My knell has rung.

Then let me waste no whimpering mood
On languid nerves and refluent blood,
But at this parting of the ways
Take counsel with my length of days.

For this is health, it seems to me,
And not an ill philosophy,
•   To rise from life's rich board before
The host can point me to the door.

So, not forgetful of the past,
Nor sulking that it could not last;
Rememb'ring, like a song's lost notes,
The gleaming husks of my wild oats;

Not, priggish, glorying in a boast
That I have never lov'd nor lost;
Not, puritanic, with a flail
Destroying others' cakes and ale;

4

In Russet and Silver

But, with new aims and hopes, prepare
To love earth less, and more haunt air;
And be as thankful as I can
To miss the beast that harries man.

Thank God, that, while the nerves decay
And muscles desiccate away,
The brain 's the hardiest part of men,
And thrives till threescore years and ten;

That, tho' the crescent flesh be wound
In soft unseemly folds around,
The heart may, all the days we live,
Grow more alert and sensitive.

Then, thews and prickly nerves, adieu!
Thanks for the years I spent with you;
Gently and cheerfully we part;
Now I must live for brain and heart.

IMPRESSION

IN these restrained and careful times
   Our knowledge petrifies our rhymes;
Ah! for that reckless fire men had
When it was witty to be mad.

When wild conceits were piled in scores,
And lit by flaring metaphors,
When all was crazed and out of tune, —
Yet throbbed with music of the moon.

If we could dare to write as ill
As some whose voices haunt us still,
Even we, perchance, might call our own
Their deep enchanting undertone.

We are too diffident and nice,
Too learned and too over-wise,
Too much afraid of faults to be
The flutes of bold sincerity.

Impression

For, as this sweet life passes by,
We blink and nod with critic eye;
We 've no words rude enough to give
Its charm so frank and fugitive.

The green and scarlet of the Park,
The undulating streets at dark,
The brown smoke blown across the blue,
This coloured city we walk through; —

The pallid faces full of pain,
The field-smell of the passing wain,
The laughter, longing, perfume, strife,
The daily spectacle of life; —

Ah! how shall this be given to rhyme,
By rhymesters of a knowing time?
Ah! for the age when verse was glad,
Being godlike, to be bad and mad.

DISCIPLINE

MY life is full of scented fruits,
   My garden blooms with stocks and cloves;
Yet o'er the wall my fancy shoots,
   And hankers after harsher loves.

' Ah! why,' — my foolish heart repines, —
   ' Was I not housed within a waste?
These velvet flowers and syrop-wines
   Are sweet, but are not to my taste.

' A howling moor, a wattled hut,
   A piercing smoke of sodden peat,
The savour of a roasted nut,
   Would make my weary pulses beat.'

O stupid brain that blindly swerves,
   O heart that strives not, nor endures,
Since flowers are hardships to your nerves,
   Thank heaven a garden-lot is yours.

A WINTER NIGHT'S DREAM

DREARY seems the task assigned me,
        Dull the play ;
I would fain leave both behind me,
        Steal away
Where no hopes nor cares could find me
        Night or day.

Where the pirate's teak prow grapples
        With pure sand,
Where Hesperidean apples
        Hem the strand,
Where the silver sunlight dapples
        Lake and land.

In some charm'd Saturnian island
        I would be ;
Watch, from glens of billowy highland,

A Winter Night's Dream

Creeks of sea ;
Crush the perfumes there awhile, and
Shake the tree.

Round the brows of naked Summer,
Noon and night,
See soft Rest, the rarest comer,
Winding bright .
Garlands that would well become her
Blithe delight.

See dusk eyes and warm brown faces
And sleek limbs
Peer from shadowy, leafy spaces;
Whence there swims
Praise to gods of unknown graces
In strange hymns.

Eat cool fruits of foreign flavour,
Drink from shells
Wine of mild, unharmful savour,
Wine that smells
Like a copse when June winds waver
All its bells.

A Winter Night's Dream

Live as live full-feeding cattle;
        Purge mine ears
From the echoing roar and rattle
        Of the years;
Then return to wholesome battle
        With my peers.

REVELATION

INTO the silver night
    She brought with her pale hand
The topaz lanthorn-light,
And darted splendour o'er the land;
    Around her in a band,
Ringstrak'd and pied, the great soft moths came flying,
    And, flapping with their mad wings, fanned
The flickering flame, ascending, falling, dying.

    Behind the thorny pink
      Close wall of blossom'd May,
    I gaz'd thro' one green chink,
And saw no more than thousands may, —
    Saw sweetness, tender and gay, —
Saw full rose lips as rounded as the cherry,
    Saw braided locks more dark than bay,
And flashing eyes, decorous, pure and merry.

Revelation

With food for furry friends,
　　She passed, her lamp and she,
　　Till eaves and gable-ends
Hid all that saffron sheen from me :
　　Around my rosy tree
Once more the silver-starry night was shining,
　　With depths of heaven, dewy and free,
And crystals of a carven moon declining.

　　Alas ! for him who dwells
　　In frigid air of thought,
　　When warmer light dispels
The frozen calm his spirit sought,
　　By life too lately taught,
He sees the ecstatic Human from him stealing ;
　　Reels from the joy experience brought,
And dares not clutch what Love was half revealing.

13

TRISTIA

CEDAR, whose boughs complain
    Soft in the sheeted rain,
Cypress, who, o'er the dead,
Noddest thy velvet head,
Oaks, thro' whose casements green
Big drops, like tears, are seen,
Yews bending to and fro,
In this wet court of woe —

Weep for the hearts that lie
Under day's maudlin eye,
Hearts that in love's red game
Leaped with the blood's bright flame,
Cared not for mist or fog,
Chirruped life's epilogue;
Now in your drip they soak —
Cedar, yew, cypress, oak!

PLAYTHINGS

THE streets are full of human toys,
  Wound up for threescore years;
Their springs are hungers, hopes and joys,
  And jealousies and fears.

They move their eyes, their lips, their hands;
  They are marvellously dressed;
And here my body stirs or stands,
  A plaything like the rest.

The toys are played with till they fall,
  Worn out and thrown away.
Why were they ever made at all?
  Who sits to watch the play?

CLASPING THE CLOUD

I YEARN not for the fighting fate,
   That holds and hath achieved,
I live to watch, and meditate
   And dream, — and be deceived.

Mine be the visionary star
   That vibrates on the sea ;
I deem Ixion happier far
   Than Jupiter could be.

NUNC DIMITTIS

IN youth our fiery lips were fed
   With fruit in lavish waste ;
We watch it now hung o'er our head, —
And, now, at length, can taste.

The boisterous pleasures of the boy
   Their own deep rapture steal ;
I ask no longer to enjoy,
   But ah ! to muse and feel.

THE SCHOOL OF FAITH

L ONG time across my path had lain
    A far-off bar like gathering rain ;
The sunshine beamed along my way,
But this drew nearer day by day.

I walked amid a laughing throng,
I plucked the flowers, I sang my song ;
But all the time my load of care,
My bar of threatening cloud, was there.

Some day, I knew, that bar must break
In tempest, fatal for my sake ;
And in my heart of hearts I laid
My secret, and was sore afraid.

And yet it caught me by surprise ;
Loud thunders pealed across the skies ;
Ere I had time for craven fear
The hour had struck. The end was near.

The School of Faith

With lips and lids set hard together
I sank upon the springy heather;
I said farewell to pleasant things,
And waited for the angel's wings.

When, oh! the marvel! through the rain
Came odours exquisite as pain;
A softer warmth, like lovers' breath,
Danced on my cheek instead of Death.

The birds around me sang in choirs;
My eyes unclosed to clearer fires;
The storm was only sent to purge
Of cloud my sky from verge to verge!

AN EVENING VOLUNTARY

A WREATH of Turkish odour winds
    Among my books in red and gold.
The philosophic spirit finds
    Peace through the pain of growing old.

The warm blue perfume melts and fades
    Around the glowing shaft of gas;
And every nervelet that upbraids
    Takes comfort from the pangs that pass.

Purer the folding air repeats
    The cones of smoke that upward slope,
And lucid grows the brain that beats
    Less turbid with the pulse of hope.

The spirals melt in fragrant mist,
    And through that mist my books shine clear;
Life dips in soberer amethyst
    The twilights of the fainting year.

An Evening Voluntary

Throb, winding belts of odorous light !
 Youth spurns me from its brilliant zest ;
But age has yet its prime delight,
 For thought survives, and thought is best.

SECRETA VITÆ

L IKE that green marble tower of yore
    From which the great carbuncle shone,
When Floris climbed to Blanchiflor
    High in the heart of Babylon, —
So steep, so smooth, so hard to reach,
The lesson only Life can teach.

She from her window, sighing, leaned
    Among the basil-pots and myrrh,
And watched those roses, daily gleaned,
    The amorous Emir sent to her ;
She sighed ; nor dreamed that rose would be
A ladder to her heart set free.

Before her door the flowers lay heaped ;
    But, heedless while she sat, and span,
Out of the trampled roses leaped
    A nameless mother-naked man ;

Secreta Vitæ

Yet o'er his shoulders straight she threw
The mantle trimmed with watchet blue.

By steps unseen, by cords unknown,
  Life scales the tower that hems our hearts;
The soul sits languid and alone,
  When, sudden, into flame it starts.
Whence came the stranger? Who can tell?
What matters, now that all is well!

Between the swallows and the stars
  To wait is all that hope can do;
Between the weary window-bars,
  To watch the fading belts of blue;
To wait, and hold a balanced mind,
Till Life his promised bride shall find.

Ah! for the simple guileless faith
  That raves not at the bolts of fate;
Ah! for the patient tongue that saith
  "Though late he cometh, not too late!"
The heart that beats in coolest rhyme
With "God's good time," and "in God's good
    time."

Secreta Vitæ

Here in my marble tower I sit ;
  Ah ! sick of pacing to and fro ;
But the hour's vast ruddy lamp is lit
  And stains with rose the world below ;
He surely comes ! the night-air sings
With tremors of his rushing wings !

Long sought, long dreamed of, long withstood,
  Cajoled by youth, and foiled by sin,
Ethereal Love ! immortal Good !
  O, thine own pathway to me win ;
Nor let me faint in hopeless strife,
Until I clasp the core of life !

Poems of Experience

A TRAGEDY WITHOUT WORDS

PASSION no more in these last days requires
   The old stock-rant of vows and darts and fires ;
We quit the frantic stage, and turn to see
A finer art, a tenderer mimicry,
But find, as through this subtler world we rove,
That, tho' a sworn Carthusian, love is Love.

Hear, in a house of peaceful days and nights,
Full of sequestered virtues, cold delights,
How two young souls could, unsuspected, fashion
A long-drawn elfin tragedy of passion.
No vows were made, no sealèd springs were broken,
No kiss was given, no word of love was spoken ;
Among calm faces clustered round the fire,
These two played out their drama of desire.

27

A Tragedy Without Words

Who knows what unseen prompter pulled the strings?
What curtain sank and wrapped them round with wings?
Not Bion, not Sebaste! Yet they know
A wild wind drove their spirits to and fro,
Swept by, — and left them, when it passed away,
Two weary actors in a finished play.

Heaven, air, and earth, spectators nothing loth,
Hung at their lips, surmised, and watched them both;
What did the March grey sky divine at length
In that sparse wood where the wind spent its strength?
Each twig of ash, contorted, tipped with black,
Whipped Bion on, and strained him at the rack;
Each primrose, darting from the arms of Death,
Dazzled Sebaste, caught her panting breath;
He plucked a flower, and with a masking jest
Craved leave to lay it on her silken breast;
She laughed, but though they both dissembled well,
One act was over, and the curtain fell.

Now thro' that noiseless house by day and night
The keen electric storm rose to its height.
What beating hearts, what dewy-glistening eyes,
What breathless questions, what demure replies!

A Tragedy Without Words

The scented twirls of wood-smoke, thin and blue,
Straight to their inmost souls like incense flew ;
When the logs fell, they started as from sleep,
Watched o'er the hearth the smouldering ruin creep,
Stole glances, met in lightning, sped apart, —
Each sitting languid with a throbbing heart.

So runs another aft ; next morning, see
Another aftor, and their parts are three !
That blue-grey form ! that rich and jetty throat !
Hark ! from a russet breast that liquid note !
How like a flash the redstart's sudden flight
Darts warm with love across Sebaste's sight !
How sleek the wings which back discreetly move, —
Like Bion's thoughts that hover round his love !
The shapely bird, those thorny boughs between,
Pours out his song, a god from a machine,
Folds and unfolds his twinkling tail in sport,
Twits now a challenge, now a brisk retort,
And makes the lover-pair so fiercely glad
That they could die for joy, — they feel so sad.

But when the snow along the woodland crest
Caught them at dusk, their pain was worst and best.

A Tragedy Without Words

Within Sebaste's heart the flood rose higher,
A keener perfume whirled across the pyre;
She felt his breath along her cheek, and glanced
Sidelong, where on dark air his profile danced;
Her hand lay tingling on his bended arm,
Each finger thrilled to find the sleeve so warm,
While down her shell-pink cheek, severe and pure,
Long lashes drooped with maiden mirth demure.

This was the hour! but Bion's swifter heat
Outstepped his pulse, and flung him at her feet,
Tame with excess of boldness just when she
Was ready for the mutual mastery;
The longed-for moment in the sparkling air,
The frost which twinkled in her tawny hair,
The gathering nonchalance in maiden blood, —
All, all were wasted on his flagging mood;
The spent bow twanged not, and 't was all in vain
Sebaste smiled on his uncouth disdain;
He found no words, till she began to link
A scarlet anger with her white and pink,
And then — 't was worse than none; and dull and
    wan
Back thro' the whitening woods went maid and man.

A Tragedy Without Words

That night the frosty world was whelmed in rain,
With restless hand wearying the window-pane ;
Deep in each silent twilight chamber lay
A heart that weighed the fortunes of the day ;
Slowly the blank night wasted ; sleep at last
Cooled each loud pulse, and closed each eyelid fast.

Sebaste waked ; the pale blue sky peeped in
And helped the cool transition to begin ;
Within her breast the night's cold seal had set
Its deep conviction, " Better to forget " ;
The hour of joyous abnegation past,
The virginal reaction fall'n at last,
She, looking back in wonder at the stir
Of pulses thrilled, held them no part of her,
And pressed her slender wrists with joy to find
Herself restored to her own quiet mind.
Bion, meanwhile, blushing with rage, rehearsed
The uncaptured hour, and his false coldness curst,
Ran o'er the tortures of the dark, and found
No ambush from the archers' stalking ground, —
No ambush except one, the vow to borrow
From last night's weakness strength to win the
    morrow,

A Tragedy Without Words

Nor ever battled in so brave a heat
As now, upon the sting of his defeat.

They met afar.   Loathing his faint disdain,
With passion seven times heated in his brain,
Bion gazed humbly at her distant eyes,
Noted her questions, weighed her light replies,
Marked when she rose, and joined her at the lawn,
Voiceless, by cords of tender longing drawn.

Silent they stood; then, thro' their lack of speech
Nature once more revealed them each to each.
Close to their very feet a squirrel came,
With feathery tail whisking his ears of flame,
Seized in pink fingers nuts and shreds of cake,
Then in long leaps raced downward to the lake.
Ah ! who shall say what bond the creature broke ?
What in that moment as in thunder spoke ?
Each turned and saw the other's soul unveiled,
Each one the other's secret being scaled ;
She read his passion, penitent and wroth,
And pitied, — as a star might watch a moth ;
He marked her cold conviction, and fell back,
As slips a boulder on a mountain track.

A Tragedy Without Words

The play was done, and after one short sigh,
He stretched his hand to her with but " Good-bye ! "
She took it, and — such mercy Heaven extends —
Held it one moment longer than a friend's ;
Then on the wet bright sward they turned and went
Self-sentenced each to mutual banishment.

MÁNES, THE HERETIC

TO J. L., DE T.

DARK, dark at last! and this warm tide of
    scent, —
A west wind in a cedarn element, —
These cold leaves of the lily out of sight,
And the long single ray of sacred light!

'T is night, then ; I have slept, and o'er my sleep
The soul of love has hovered close and deep.

A bat moves in the porphyry capitals,
And cuts the clear-drawn radiance as it falls ;
So man, intruding in his bestial way,
Shears from the lamp of God the heavenly ray.

Ah ! to my keen and tempered senses rise
The temple-perfumes like a people's cries, —
The cinnamon, a prayer beneath the stars,
Adoring love pulsed from the nenuphars,

Manes, the Heretic

Sharp aloes, like a soul that strives with sin,
And myrrh, the song of one all chaste within ;
In each I join, on each my spirit flies
To float, a thread of mist, along the skies.

By every way we soar to God's abode,
But rising perfumes pave the smoothest road.

Hail ! Soul of all things, parted, yet not lost,
One sea of myriad breakers torn and tost,
One river eastward, westward, northward bent
And branching through a monstrous continent,
Yet drawn at last by every winding road
Down to that noiseless marish which is God !
Thou art the wind that like a player's hand
Strikes out harp-music where these columns stand,
Thou art the small hushed cry of crisp dry life
The terebinth gives beneath the carver's knife,
And the soft alabaster sighs for thee
When the pale sculptor shreds it on his knee.

I pluck these fig-leaves, broad, and smooth as silk,
And godhead weeps from them in tears of milk ;
I catch those fish of glimmering fin and tail,
And godhead sparkles from each fading scale.

Manes, the Heretic

I draw the Indian curtain from my bed,
And Thou the lustrous arch above my head;
It falls in folds, and this one beam I see,
O tender heavenly Light, is trebly Thee!

Ah! Thou, invoked by many a mystic sign,
Bend hither from Thy secret crystalline,
O'er Thy twin angels' arms be seen to move,
Let Light and Perfume teach me Thou art Love.
In this dusk world of scentless, hueless man
My soul once heard Thee, and to light it ran,
Shot leaf and bud from out its watery bed,
And in adoring fragrance Thee-ward spread.
Then Thy soft ray, ineffable, divine,
Flushed my cold petals with ecstatic wine,
The pistils trembled, and the stamens flew
Straight to the centre, where their god they knew,
Clung quivering there, enkindled and a-glow,
Sank, big with blessing, on the leaves below;
I bowed, — and, deep within my soul I found
A fount of balm for dying worlds around.

And now, within the temple they have built,
I live to expiate a nation's guilt;

Manes, the Heretic

To me they blindly pray, I handing on
To Thee the essence of each orison.

I bask within one narrow'd beam all day,
And sleep all night within this single ray ;
While, like the sound of many an instrument,
Floats round me ever this rich tide of scent.
So may I live till all my dreams are o'er,
Then on a shaft of radiance upward soar,
Fade as a thread of dew the sun draws up,
And, kindled high in heaven's inverted cup,
Like some aroma melt into the sense
Of Thy supine and cold omnipotence.

THE NEW MEMNON

TO A. L.

WHEN with hammers of iron Cambyses had
broken
The statue of Memnon that sang to the sun,
And the desolate marble no longer gave token
That twilight was ended and dawn had begun,
The priesthood who long had been punctual and
choral
To wait on their god as the stars waned away,
Drowsed on in their beds while the clouds flushed
auroral,
Or droned in the desecrate temple of Day.

So the slow wave of fashion ebbed down from the
wonder,
And worshippers failed at the bountiful shrine, —
Where never the shock of the sun aroused thunder,
Or music welled forth from the stone un-divine;

38

The New Memnon

Yet, when all had deserted, one chieftain came creeping
  Through reeds and through grasses where Memnon
    lay bare,
Night after dull night, when the priests were all
    sleeping,
  Came yearning and dreaming, and dared not despair.

To him, so the tale runs, one morning when slender
  The naked beam flushed on the shattered white
    stone,
A word came in message, so thrilling, so tender,
  It sobbed like a harp-string that dies in a moan ;
" My son ! all is done, all is done ! " and so ended ;
  He fell on his face, and, by gift of the god,
In the growing blue blaze of day, African, splendid,
  His heart sank as cold as the granite he trod.

So be it with all of my being that 's mortal,
  If ever that tyrant, the World, should destroy
The wonderful image which stands at my portal
  And sings to my spirit of hope and of joy ;
When the rose-flame of thought on that marble illusion
  Rings music no more from its sensitive heart,

The New Memnon

When I've waited and watched, and the faithful
    delusion
    Sighs forth a farewell, and I feel it depart ; —

Ah ! then in the gloom of my broken ideal,
    In the concave moon-shadow away from the sun,
When the horrors of earth are grown rugged and real,
    By some fortunate stroke may my coil be undone ;
Ah ! better to pass to the sullen dumb hollows
    Where sounds never jar on the ear of the dead,
Than to learn that the air which my destiny follows
    By some trick of a huckster was fostered and fed.

CHATTAFIN

I.

MY orchard blooms with high September light,
    Opal and topaz star the burning grass ;
The hedgerow-fluted meadows climb the height,
    And into gulfs of silver'd azure pass ;
The glittering hawk-weed turns to golden glass
The dew'd enamel of the rough pale field ;
    With laden boughs, a lichen-hoary mass,
Rolls the arch'd canopy of autumn's yield,
And hides a liquid gloom beneath its leafy shield.

II.

Come to me now, while all the winds are dumb,
    And, floating in this earthly hyaline,
Bring me no whisper of the harsh world's hum,
    But, with an indolence attuned to mine,

Chattafin

Pass to my soul the thoughts that wave in thine;
Like those twin brooks that stir our field below
    Whose sparkles meet in music; they divine
No first nor second place, but all they know
Is that with doubled strength they seaward leap and
    flow.

.

III.

Come to me now; come from the mart of men,
    To this monastic court of apple-trees.
See, the grey heron rises from the fen,
    And mark! his slower mate by long degrees
    Follows and flaps to stiller shades than these;
They wing their lonesome meditative way
    To some hush'd elbow of the reedy leas;
O let us lose ourselves in flight, as they
Their heart's sequestered law thus tenderly obey.

IV.

Here all is gained we waste our lives demanding;
    Here all things meet that, feverish, we pursue;
The peace of God that passeth understanding
    Falls on this place, and, like a chrism of dew,

Chattafin

Without a murmur, steeps us thro' and thro';
Here hopes are pure, and aims are cool and high;
  Here Pisgah-glints of Heaven may greet our
  view;
O come and in green light of glory lie,
And talk of song and death, without or flush or sigh.

THE WOUNDED GULL

TO P. H. G., JR.

A LONG a grim and granite shore
With children and with wife I went,
And in our face the stiff breeze bore
Salt savours and a samphire scent.

So wild the place and desolate,
That on a rock before us stood - -
All upright, silent and sedate —
Of dark-grey gulls a multitude.

The children could not choose but shout
To see these lovely birds so near,
Whereat they spread their pinions out,
Yet rather in surprise than fear.

44

The Wounded Gull

They rose and wheeled around the cape,
   They shrieked and vanished in a flock;
But lo! one solitary shape
   Still sentinelled the lonely rock.

The children laughed, and called it tame!
   But ah! one dark and shrivell'd wing
Hung by its side; the gull was lame,
   A suffering and deserted thing.

With painful care it downward crept;
   Its eye was on the rolling sea;
Close to our very feet, it stept
   Upon the wave, and then — was free.

Right out into the east it went,
   Too proud, we thought, to flap or shriek;
Slowly it steered, in wonderment
   To find its enemies so meek.

Calmly it steered, and mortal dread
   Disturbed nor crest nor glossy plume;
It could but die, and being dead,
   The open sea should be its tomb.

The Wounded Gull

We watched it till we saw it float
  Almost beyond our furthest view ;
It flickered like a paper boat,
  Then faded in the dazzling blue.

It could but touch an English heart,
  To find an English bird so brave ;
Our life-blood glowed to see it start
  Thus boldly on the leaguered wave ;

And we shall hold, till life departs,
  For flagging days when hope grows dull,
Fresh as a spring within our hearts,
  The courage of the wounded gull.

THE PRODIGAL

WHEN life is young, and all the world seems
waiting
To crown the bright prince Self, his bondage done,
The callow eager heart feels no debating,
But takes affection as flowers drink the sun.

A little while, he saith, and men must know me;
A few feet more, and I must reach the light;
The private love these homely bosoms show me
Perchance may lift me into public sight.

But ah ! time slowly strips the vain illusion,
And decks the fairy prince in common clothes;
The breathless ages prove a boy's delusion,
And nought so faithless as the Muses' oaths.

When battling hopes that made the fresh pulse martial,
Spring up no more behind the fife and drum,

47

The Prodigal

Success may come, yet cropped and tame and partial,
    And joys, — but life has faded ere they come;

Then in that pause, when pride has lost its splendour,
    When foiled ambition smiles itself to sleep,
Back rush old thoughts, familiar thoughts and tender,
    That slumber'd in the conscience, dumb and deep.

Then all the withered loves that once fell fading,
    Stir like long weeds below a tidal sea;
Then all the thankless past returns upbraiding, —
    Then all my memory turns in shame to thee.

The trustful bird close to thy window flutters,
    The squirrel takes his breakfast from thy hand,
And every accent that thy whisper utters
    Thrill the meek subjects of thy garden-land.

Thou hast the crafty voice, the magic fingers
    That round the woodland pulse have art to twine,
Yet oft I think, among thy serfs and singers,
    The wildest capture was this heart of mine.

The Prodigal

Ah ! take me home ; my pride of pinion broken,
  My song untuned, my morning-light decayed !
I bring thee back thine own old love for token
  That I am he for whom it toiled and prayed.

Undone the toil, and vain the intercession !
  But ah ! beneath thy fire for my success
There lurked a hungry sense of lost possession
  And for my failure thou 'lt not love me less.

Dear ! for my sake the streets will ne'er be lighted ;
  The Senate never ring with cheers for me !
Open thy garden-gate to one benighted,
  And take me safely back to peace and thee. -

D

AN ENGLISH VILLAGE

(SNOWSHILL)

THERE lies a vale in Cotswold still as death
And empty as the sky, a grey cold dale,
That pours its labour forth at break of day,
And hears no sound nor beating at its heart
Till toil creeps back at sundown.
                                    Walls of stone
Of immemorial age, yet unembossed
With lichen or with rue-worth, nurse its hearths
Of trembling embers.   O'er its box-tree walks
The twinkling martins cut their subtle rings.

Here yellow apples glow, like myriad lamps,
On strained and drooping branches, tier by tier,
Drawn up the wold in wasting orchards grey.

Nothing is here that was not here and thus
When Milton shook his long ambrosial curls

An English Village

O'er Cromwell's rough state-papers, nothing here
The chanting Roundhead hath not seen and felt
Riding from Worcester to his woodland home
On Evenlode or Windrush.

                     Here at least
Nature and Man have grown so like each other,
In close perennial concert, that the voice
Of one is as the other's.

                     Miles away
I hear faint bayings of the Broadway hounds:
The hunt is up, — it will not reach us here!
Here are no louder sounds than, drop by drop,
The patient trickling that a water-thread
Makes down the clouded well.   No bird, no boy,
No whirring insect with a strident wing,
Transgresses the rich vow of tongueless peace.
Here even a hermit's heart might break at last;
All is too still ; and Solitude herself
Would chafe against so cold a chain of stone.

Even as I gaze, it grows intolerable !
October lingered in one last red rose,
But as the light breeze rises, at my feet
Lo ! these last petals in a crimson shower

An English Village

Lie fallen.   Winter, like a felon ghost,
That with its viewless presence chills the blood,
Has slipped upon us from the hoary wold ;
I fly, and leave the vale beneath his sway
As tranquil as a sea without a wave.

NEURASTHESIA

Non malattia mortale,
Mà fu celeste forza ;
Non propria ellitione,
Mà un impeto fatal.

SPERONE.

C URS'D from the cradle and awry they come,
　　Masking their torment from a world at ease ;
On eyes of dark entreaty, vague and dumb,
　　They bear the stigma of their souls' disease.

Bewildered by the shadowy ban of birth,
　　They learn that they are not as others are,
Till some go mad, and some sink prone to earth,
　　And some push stumbling on without a star ;

And some, of sterner mould, set hard their hearts,
　　To aft the dreadful comedy of life,
And wearily grow perfeft in their parts ; —
　　But all are wretched and their years are strife.

Neurasthesia

The common cheer that animates mankind,
    The tender general comfort of the race,
To them is colour chattered to the blind,
    A book held up against a sightless face.

Like sailors drifting under cliffs of steel,
    Whose fluttering magnets leap with lying poles,
They doubt the truth of every law they feel,
    And Death yawns for them if they trust their souls.

The loneliest creatures in the wash of air,
    They search the world for solace, but in vain ;
No priest rewards their confidence with prayer,
    And no physician remedies their pain.

Ah ! let us spare our wrath for these, forlorn,
    Nor chase a bubble on the intolerant wave ;
Let pity quell the gathering storm of scorn,
    And God, who made them so, may soothe and
        save.

Lyrics

ALERE FLAMMAM

TO A. C. B.

IN ancient Rome, the secret fire, —
    An intimate and holy thing, —
Was guarded by a tender choir
    Of kindred maidens in a ring;
Deep, deep within the home it lay,
    No stranger ever gazed thereon,
But, flickering still by night and day,
    The beacon of the house, it shone;
Thro' birth and death, from age to age,
It passed, a quenchless heritage;

And there were hymns of mystic tone
    Sung round about the family flame,
Beyond the threshold all unknown,
    Fast-welded to an ancient name;

Alere Flammam

There sacrificed the sire as priest,
　Before that altar, none but he,
Alone he spread the solemn feast
　For a most secret deity ;
He knew the god had once been sire,
And served the same memorial fire.

Ah ! so, untouched by windy roar
　Of public issues loud and long,
The Poet holds the sacred door,
　And guards the glowing coal of song ;
Not his to grasp at praise or blame,
　Red gold, or crowns beneath the sun,
His only pride to tend the flame
　That Homer and that Virgil won,
Retain the rite, preserve the act,
And pass the worship on intact.

Before the shrine at last he falls ;
　The crowd rush in, a chattering band ;
But, ere he fades in death, he calls
　Another priest to ward the brand ;
He, with a gesture of disdain,

Alere Flammam

Flings back the ringing brazen gate,
Reproves, repressing, the profane,
    And feeds the flame in primal state ;
Content to toil and fade in turn
If still the sacred embers burn.

THE SWAN

THE awakening swan grows tired at last
  Of weltering pastures where he feeds;
With wings and feet behind him cast,
  He cleaves the labyrinth of reeds.

He arches out his sparkling plumes,
  He wades and plunges, till he finds
Beneath his breast the azure glooms
  Where the great river brims and winds.

Then, with white sails set to the breeze,
  The current cold about his feet,
He fares to those Hesperides
  Where morning and his comrades meet.

Nor — since within his kindling veins
  A livelier ichor stirs at last —
Regrets the gross and juicy stains,
  The saps and savours of the past;

The Swan

But through the august and solemn void
  Of misty waters holds his way,
By some ecstatic thirst decoyed
  Towards raptures of the radiant day.

So sails the soul, and cannot rest,
  Inglorious, in the marsh of peace,
But leaves the good, to seek the best,
  Though all its calms and comforts cease, —

Though what it seemed to hold be lost,
  Though that grow far which once was nigh, —
By torturing hope in anguish tossed,
  The awakened soul must sail or die.

THE WALL-PAPER

WHEN I was only five years old,
  My mother, who was soon to die,
Raised me with fingers soft and cold,
    On high ;

Until, against the parlour wall,
  I reached a golden paper flower.
How proud was I, and ah ! how tall,
    That hour !

" This shining tulip shall be yours,
  Your own, your very own," she said ;
The mark that made it mine endures
    In red.

I scarce could see it from the floor ;
  I craned to touch the scarlet sign ;
No gift so precious had before
    Been mine.

The Wall-Paper

A paper tulip on a wall !
A boon that ownership defied !
Yet this was dearer far than all
      Beside.

Real toys, real flowers that lavish love
      Had strewn before me, all and each
Grew pale beside this gift above
      My reach.

Ah ! now that time has worked its will,
      And fooled my heart, and dazed my eyes,
Delusive tulips prove me still
      Unwise.

Still, still the eluding flower that glows
      Above the hands that yearn and clasp
Seems brighter than the genuine rose
      I grasp.

So has it been since I was born ;
      So will it be until I die ;
Stars, the best flowers of all, adorn
      The sky.

THE NAUTILUS

VENUS, take this shell,
  Offering of a bride !
Once it rose and fell
  On thy mooney tide ;
Let its pearly bulwarks dwell
  By thy side.

Rigged with gossamer,
  O'er thy seas it flew :
Never a wind would stir
  Cord or sail or crew ;
Halycon-like, this mariner
  Cleft the blue.

Blithe even so was I,
  Gay, light-hearted maid ;
Now my sails are dry,
  My fond crew afraid ;
Goddess, goddess ; come, I cry,
  To my aid !

The Nautilus

Is it bliss or woe,
  Nevermore to flee
O'er the full heart's flow,
  Indolent and free,
As this shell strayed long ago
  O'er the sea?

Venus, take this shell,
  Pearly like a tear!
Ah! I cannot tell
  What I wish or fear;
Guard me through the miracle,
  Dread and dear.

A DREAM OF NOVEMBER

TO A. S.

F AR, far away, I know not where, I know not how,
The skies are grey, the boughs are bare, bare
boughs in flower :
Long lilac silk is softly drawn from bough to bough,
With flowers of milk and buds of fawn, a broidered
shower.

Beneath that tent an Empress sits, with slanted eyes,
And wafts of scent from censers flit, a lilac flood ;
Around her throne bloom peach and plum in
lacquered dyes,
And many a blown chrysanthemum, and many a
bud.

She sits and dreams, while bonzes twain strike some
rich bell,
Whose music seems a metal rain of radiant dye ;

A Dream of November

In this strange birth of various blooms, I cannot tell
  Which sprang from earth, which slipped from
    looms, which sank from sky.

Beneath her wings of lilac dim, in robes of blue,
  The Empress sings a wordless hymn that thrills her
    bower;
My trance unweaves, and winds, and shreds, and
    weaves anew
  Dark bronze, bright leaves, pure silken threads, in
    triple flower.

ON YES TOR

BENEATH our feet, the shuddering bogs
    Made earthquakes of their own,
For greenish-grizzled furtive frogs
    And lizards lithe and brown.

And high to east and south and west,
    Girt round the feet with gorse,
Lay, summering, breast by giant breast,
    The Titan brood of tors;

Golden and phantom-pale they lay,
    Calm in the cloudless light,
Like gods that, slumbering, still survey
    The obsequious infinite.

Plod, plod, through herbage thin or dense,
    Past chattering rills of quartz,
Across brown bramble-coverts, whence
    The shy black ouzel darts,

On Yes•Tor

Through empty leagues of broad, bare lands,
  Beneath the empty skies,
Clutched in the grip of those vast hands,
  Cowed by those golden eyes,

We fled beneath their scornful stare,
  Like terror-hunted dogs,
More timid than the lizards were,
  And shyer than the frogs.

TO A CHILD OF FIFTEEN

JASMINE of girlhood, thou whose star —
   Unlike those planets poised afar —
Hangs near, as thou art, sweet and pure
In household foliage warm, demure ;

Take this dusk heart beneath thy sway !
Bend, graceful Jasmine, bend my way !
Thy trumpet-note of perfume blow
Across the path by which I go.

Too dry would be the dust, too harsh
The herbage of the holt and marsh,
Were there no bowers, the dewy shrine
Of homely-scented stars like thine.

Then let me by thine innocence
Be weaned from too-sagacious sense ;
Let him on whom thy flower hath smiled
Grow milkier-hearted than a child.

TO THE ALMOND

P RIEST in the masque of pleasure!
 The wind's rude hand disposes
Thy fair brow's ruffled treasure,
Thy wrecked and scattered crown of pale pink roses.

 The soft west wind comes sighing
  With weight of scents that load her;
 Spring wakes as thou art dying,
Thou harbinger of sunlight, warmth, and odour.

 Thy flower might seem the fuel
  That feeds the Spring's green taper,
 So quickly doth its jewel
From thy black branches fade away in vapour.

 So bright thy bloom and fleeting,
  So sweet and transitory,
 Our parting blends with greeting,
As fame or love with death in human story.

To the Almond

Then *ave atque vale!*
  Though thus so briefly blowing,
  Such wonders crowd us daily,
We have no heart, fair flower, to weep thy going.

  Farewell! with all thy graces!
  Till thou hast flickered by us,
  Their florid full embraces
Laburnum, chestnut, lilac, thorn, deny us.

PHILOMEL IN LONDON

TO G. A. A.

NOT within a granite pass,
    Dim with flowers and soft with grass —
Nay but doubly, trebly sweet
In a poplared London street,
While below my windows go
Noiseless barges, to and fro,
    Through the night's calm deep,
Ah ! what breaks the bonds of sleep ?

No steps on the pavement fall,
Soundless swings the dark canal ;
From a church-tower out of sight
Clangs the central hour of night.
Hark ! the Dorian nightingale !
Pan's voice melted to a wail !
    Such another bird
Attic Tereus never heard.

Philomel in London

Hung above the gloom and stain —
London's squalid cope of pain —
Pure as starlight, bold as love,
Honouring our scant poplar-grove,
That most heavenly voice of earth
Thrills in passion, grief or mirth,
      Laves our poison'd air
Life's best song-bath crystal-fair.

While the starry minstrel sings
Little matters what he brings,
Be it sorrow, be it pain ;
Let him sing and sing again,
Till, with dawn, poor souls rejoice,
Wakening, once to hear his voice,
      Ere afar he flies,
Bound for purer woods and skies.

THE IRIS

F RAIL iris, from whose fragile sheath,
    In lilac and in primrose hue,
    The beakéd bud just pushes through
    To greet the blackbirds and the blue,
What news from hollow worlds beneath ?

In strata of the kindling sod
    What murmur reached you of the spring ?
    What proof of warmth and weft and wing
    Broke through your blank imagining,
And thrilled your core with hopes of God ?

Wak'd to a rapture unaware,
    Your rootlet, iris, stirr'd with faith ;
    You caught the voice of Him who saith
    " Spring is the vapour of my breath,
And sap the sound of answered prayer."

SONG FOR MUSIC

COUNT the flashes in the surf,
  Count the crystals in the snow,
Or the blades above the turf,
  Or the dead that sleep below !
  These ye count — yet shall not know, —
While I wake or while I slumber, —
  Where my thoughts and wishes go,
What her name, and what their number.

Ask the cold and midnight sea,
  Ask the silent-falling frost,
Ask the grasses on the lea,
  Or the mad maid, passion-crost !
  They may tell of posies tost
To the waves where blossoms blow not,
  Tell of hearts that staked and lost, —
But of me and mine they know not.

HOPE DEFERRED.

FAINT lines of grey are in that hair
    That was one year ago so fair,
So curl'd in gold, so wav'd with light,
And still the feathery hours flit by,
And we grow older, you and I,
And still I wait for your reply,
    And all your answer still is flight.

You touch my hand a little while,
You pierce me with your flashing smile,
    You dart away, away, away !
O for the skill to hold you fast,
O for the art to win at last
One sunset hour ere life be past,
    One thrill before the nerves decay.

TO A TRAVELLER.

From the Greek.

AFTER many a dusty mile,
  Wanderer, linger here awhile ;
Stretch your limbs in dewy grass ;
Through these pines a wind shall pass
That shall cool you with its wing ;
Grasshoppers shall shout and sing ;
While the shepherd on the hill,
Near a fountain warbling still,
Modulates, when noon is mute,
Summer songs along his flute ;
Underneath a spreading tree,
None so easy-limbed as he,
Sheltered from the dog-star's heat.

Rest ; and then, on freshened feet,
You shall pass the forest through.
It is Pan that counsels you.

THE FIELDFARE'S NEST

TO E. B.

THOUGH all should smile denying, I believe
    These elms have borne the Fieldfare's fabulous
    nest.
Why else in England should he build and rest,
Quitting the flock in which his brethren leave

Our shores forsaken on an April eve,
    Save, on these lawns, to preen a speckled breast,
    And hear your feathery friends proclaim you blest?
Where else so safe a bower could Fieldfare weave?

· The Fieldfare's Nest

Ah ! might he borrow notes as sweet as those
  With which the Mavis pays you all day long
  (Our delicate Mavis with her slighted song),
You would not doubt the enchanted Fieldfare knows
This magic garden's secret of repose,
  And reads her heart to whom these glades belong.

SHUT OF EVE

OUR long, long day of warmth is done;
    Take courage to depart;
The world is chill without the sun,
    My heart, without thy heart.

In vaporous air the willows waved,
    Like sea-weeds in the sea;
No other boon my spirit craved
    Than life, warm life with thee.

The glimmering corner of our lake
    Still glows with amber light;
The cold soft tops of grasses break
    Our long low line of sight.

But all in vain; like dying eyes
    That watch in hopeless hope,
We think to change with prayers and sighs
    Our fatal horoscope.

Shut of Eve

An hour of sun, an hour of breeze,
  An hour of passionate love ;
And then the night, and moaning trees,
  And folded skies above.

So let us sigh " Farewell ! bright day,
  Warm fern, and grassy dell ;
The day is done, then let's away !
  Day, life, hope, love, farewell ! "

THE POPLAR TREE

HERE, underneath this poplar tree,
        Long years ago,
My life flowed fast, as rivers flow
        To sea.

That day, when thought and passion flew
        On eagle wings,
The smooth sky, tuned to calmer things,
        Was blue.

To-day, while numb with dull distress,
        My pulse sinks dead ;
The heavens are azure overhead
        Not less.

The Poplar Tree

O shivering, laughing poplar tree,
    .   Till I came here
The world held less of hope and fear
              For me!

Ye silvery heavens, cease to shine!
        Sigh, poplar, sigh!
The body of death that passeth by
        Is mine.

CIRCLING FANCIES

A ROUND this tree the floating flies
    Weave their mysterious webs of light ;
The scent of my acacia lies
    Within the circle of their flight ;
    They never perch nor drop from sight,
But, flashing, wheel in curves of air,
    As if the perfume's warm delight
In magic bondage held them there.

I watch them till I half confound
    Their motion, with these thoughts of mine
That no less subtle bonds have bound
    Within a viewless ring divine ;
    Clasped by a chain that makes no sign
My hopes and wheeling fancies live ;
    Desires, like odours, still confine
The heart that else were fugitive.

85

Circling Fancies

Then flash and float thro' tides of June,
  Ye summer phantoms of my love!
Let all the woodlands join in tune
  While on your gauzy wings ye move!
  With odour round, and light above,
Your aery symbol-circle keep,
  Till night descends; then may I prove
More constant, circling still in sleep.

LOVE–LETTERS

I 'VE learned, in dream or legend dark,
That all love-letters purged with fire,
Drawn in one constellated spark,
To heaven aspire.

To-night there streams across the sky
An unfamiliar reef of stars ;
Are those the letters you and I
Thrust through the bars ?

In tears of joy they once were read,
In tears of suffering slowly burned ;
And now to stars hung overhead
Can each be turned ?

O leaves too warm to be discreet,
O panting words that throbbed too loud,
With starry laughter now you meet
Behind a cloud !

Love–Letters

You watch us sleeping all night long,
  Until grey morning bids you fade ;
You charge us, with your choral song,
  Be undismayed !

Alas ! the Magians knew your names,
  Ye ancient lamps of amber light ;
'T is vanity of passion claims
  So rare delight.

We might as well lay claim to Mars ! —
  And yet — I surely understand
That softest yellow flashing star's
  Italian hand ?

Memorial Verses

IN POETS' CORNER

WHEN first the clamorous poets sang, and when,
    Acclaim'd by hosts of men,
While music filled with silver light and shade
    Cloister and colonnade,
With pomp of catafalque and laureate crown
    We laid him softly down
To sleep until the world's last morning come,
    My stricken lips were dumb.

But now that all is silent round his grave,
    Dim, from the glimmering nave,
And in the shadow thrown by plinth and bust
    His garlands gather dust,
Here, in the hush, I feel the chords unstrung
    Tighten in throat and tongue ;
At last, at last, the voice comes back, — I raise
    A whisper in his praise.

In Poet's Corner

Thanks for the music that through thirty years
    Quicken'd my pulse to tears,
The eye that colour'd nature, the wise hand,
    The brain that nobly plann'd ;
Thanks for the anguish of the perfect phrase.
    Tingling the blood ablaze !
Organ of God, with multitudinous swell
    Of various tone, farewell !

BALLADE

FOR THE FUNERAL OF THE LAST OF THE

JOYOUS POETS

ONE ballade more before we say good-night,
     O dying Muse, one mournful ballade more!
Then let the new men fall to their delight,
     The Impressionist, the Decadent, a score
     Of other fresh fanatics, who adore
Quaint demons, and disdain thy golden shrine;
Ah! faded goddess, thou wert held divine
     When we were young! But now each laurelled head
Has fallen, and fallen the ancient glorious line;
     The last is gone, since Banville too is dead.

Peace, peace a moment, dolorous Ibsenite!
     Pale Tolstoist, moaning from the Euxine shore!
Psychology, to dreamland take thy flight!
     And, fell Heredity, forbear to pour
     Drop after drop thy dose of hellebore,

Ballade

For we look back to-night to ruddier wine
And gayer singing than these moans of thine !
   Our skies were azure once, our roses red,
Our poets once were crowned with eglantine ;
The last is gone, since Banville too is dead.

With flutes and lyres and many a lovely rite
   Through the mad woodland of our youth they bore
Verse, like pure ichor in a chrysolite,
   Secret yet splendid, and the world forswore,
   For one brief space, the mocking mask it wore.
Then failed, then fell those children of the vine, —
Sons of the sun, — and sank in slow decline ;
   Pulse after pulse their radiant lives were shed ;
To silence we their vocal names consign ;
   The last is gone, since Banville too is dead.

ENVOI

PRINCE-JEWELLER, whose facet-rhymes combine
All hues that glow, all rays that shift and shine,
   Farewell ! thy song is sung, thy splendour fled !
No bards to Aganippe's wave incline ;
   The last is gone, since BANVILLE too is dead.

ANNE CLOUGH

Feb. 28, 1892

ESTEEM'D, admir'd, belov'd, — farewell!
Alas! what need hadst thou of peace?
Our bitterest winter tolls the knell,
And tolls, and tolls, and will not cease.

It tolls and tolls with iron tongue
For empty lives and hearts unbless'd,
And tolls for thee, whose heart was young,
Whose life was stored with hope and rest.

Thy meditative quaint replies,
Cast out like arrows on the air,
The humour in thy dark blue eyes,
The wisdom in thy silver hair,

Tho' these grow faint, shade after shade,
As those who loved thee droop and pass, ·

Anne Clough

Thy being was not wholly made
  To shrink like breath upon a glass.

Thou with new graces didst maintain
  The old, outworn scholastic seat,
Throned, simply, with an ardent train
  Of studious beauty round thy feet.

Those girls, grown mothers soon, will teach
  Their sons to praise thy sacred name,
Thy hand that taught their hands to reach
  The broader thought, the brighter flame.

So thou, tho' sunk amidst the gloom
  That gathers round our reedy shore,
Shalt with diffusèd light illume
  A thousand hearths unlit before.

BEATRICE

THRO' Dante's hands, in dreamy vigil clasp'd
  A pale green bud shot skyward from the sod ;
He bowed and sighed ; then laid the prize he grasp'd,
  A folded lily, at the feet of God.

There she hath slowly open'd, age by age,
  And grown a star to light Man's heart to heaven ;
Her perfume his divinest heritage,
  Her love the noblest gift God's self hath given.

BLAKE

THEY win who never near the goal,
    They run who halt on wounded feet;
Art hath its martyrs like the soul,
    Its victors in defeat.

This seer's ambition soar'd too far ;
    He sank, on pinions backward blown ;
But, tho' he touched nor sun nor star,
    He made a world his own.

DANTE GABRIEL ROSSETTI

A LL pomps and gorgeous rites, all visions old,
Nursed by the ancient Spouse of Christ serene
Within the solemn precincts of her fold,
   To him were dear, as angel-wings once seen
Across a ruin'd minster's spires of gold
   To some old priest in exile might have been.

The gloom, the splendour of the apse, the cloud
   Of streaming incense swung aloft the choir,
The murmuring organ, muffled now, now loud,
   The great rose-window like a flower on fire,
The choral shout, the countless faces bowed, —
   These were the plectrum and his soul the lyre.
In leaving these he wrought his instinct wrong, —
   He sprang from no protesting ancestry ;

Dante Gabriel Rossetti

'Those ancient signs of worship waked his song,
  And though a pagan he might feign to be,
In Arcady he never wandered long,
  Nor truly loved the goddess of the sea.

His mighty spirit was an outlaw yet
  In this bright garish modern life of ours ;
His statue should with Gothic kings' be set,
  Engarlanded with saints and carven flowers,
Or on some dim Italian altar, wet
  With votive tears and sprinkled hyssop-showers.

He is made one with all the Easter fires,
  With all the perfume and the rainbow-light,
His voice is mingled with the ascending choir's,
  Broken and spent through traceries infinite ;
Above the rich triforium, past the spires,
  The answering music melts into the night.

Farewell ! though time hath vanquished our desire,
  We shall not be as though he had not been ;
Some love of mystic thought in strange attire,
  Of things unseen reflected in the seen,
Of heights towards which the sons of flesh aspire,
  Shall haunt us with a yearning close and keen.

Dante Gabriel Rossetti

Farewell! upon the marble of his tomb
  Let some great sculptor carve a knight in prayer,
Who dreams he sees the holy vision come.
  Now let the night-wind pass across his hair;
Him can no more vain backward hope consume,
  Nor the world vex him with her wasting care.

Easter Sunday, 1882.

JOHN HENRY NEWMAN

August 11, 1890

PEACE to the virgin heart, the crystal brain!
 Truce for one hour thro' all the camps of
 thought!
Our subtlest mind hath rent the veil of pain,
 Hath found the truth he sought.

Who knows what script those opening eyes have read?
 If this set creed, or that, or none be best?
Let no strife jar above this snow-white head!
 Peace for a saint at rest!

TO JENNY LIND

THEY call thee Nightingale, who know thee
    not!
But Philomel's light voice within her tree
Betrays an instinct of her transient lot; '
    As flowers to gems are, so are birds to thee.

LECONTE DE LISLE

July 17, 1894

HIS verse was carved in ivory forms, undying
As those that deck the marble Phidian
frieze.
Over his plaintive hearse to-night is flying
A phantom genius from the Cyclades.

It hovers till our idle rites be over;
And then will bear him in its arms away
To islands cinctured by the sun, their lover,
And spicy woodlands thrilled with fiery day.

There his dark hours of toil shall drop, forgotten;
There all he loved, simple and calm and grand —
All the white creatures by his Muse begotten —
Shall cluster round him in a stately band.

Leconte de Lisle

Then shall he smile, appeased by sovereign beauty,
  Contented that he strove and waited long,
Since in those worlds where loveliness is duty
  His bronze and marble leap to life and song.

MADRIGAL

SET FORTH TO BE SUNG TO THE BASS VIOL IN
PRAISE OF MR. BULLEN HIS EDITION OF
THE WORDS OF DR. THOMAS CAMPION

HE comes again !
  The latest, not the least desired !
    Too long in mouldering tomes retired,
We sought in vain
Those breathing airs
    Which, from his instrument,
    Like vocal winds of perfume, blent
To soothe man's piercing cares.

BULLEN, well done !
    Where Campion lies in London-land,
    Lulled by the thunders of the Strand,

Madrigal

Screened from the sun,
Surely there must
    Now pass some pleasant gleam
    Across his music-haunted dream
Whose brain and lute are dust.

WITH A COPY OF
SHAKESPEARE'S SONNETS

THIS is the holy missal Shakespeare wrote,
 For friends to ponder when they grieve
  alone ;
Within these collects his great heart would note
 Its joy and fear, its ecstasy and moan ;
Our strength and weakness each was felt by him ;
 He yearned and shrank, rejoiced and hoped and
  bled ;
Nor ever will his sacred song be dim,
 Though he himself, the Friend of Friends, is dead.
Then, on sad evenings when you think of me,
 Or when the morn seems blithe, yet I not near,
Open this book, and read, and I shall be
 The metre murmuring at your bended ear :
I cannot write my love with Shakespeare's art,
But the same burden weighs upon my heart.

Miscellany Poems

THE WITCHES

I.

AT dead of night in Cranley street.
    A silent crowd of yokels meet ;
In marshalled line they form, and stand
With candles lighted in their hand ;
Then up the lane they turn to go :
Down the calm mead no breezes blow,
The flame scarce wavers to and fro —
    The flame to scare the witches.

II.

And now, through smoke of flaring dips,
The stars are seen, like ghostly ships,
With all sails set in heaven's dark sea ;
And ghostly white from the elder-tree
The clusters hang ; but still there flows
No honey from the parched-up rose,
No breath from the honeysuckle blows —
    All 's blighted by the witches.

The Witches

Through leaden air the young men pass,
Their shoes are dry in the long grass;
No living creature round them stirs,
No weasel squeaks, no fern-owl whirrs,
Through the dark night with might and main —
Each nerve and sinew on the strain —
They bear their candles up the lane
To daunt the midnight witches.

IV.

But one by one their flames burn blue,
And all but three, then all but two,
By unseen lips at gateways blown,
Go out, till one is left alone;
One trembling flame that seems to shrink
Within its cage of fingers pink,
And now would rise and now would sink,
Sole help against the witches.

V.

Still guarding this one light they rise,
Till, darker than the dark blue skies,
The windmill upon Coneyhurst,
A starless shape above them burst;

The Witches

And through the fern and furze they hear,
With aching nerve of the tingling ear,
A sound that curdles them with fear, —
    The rustling of the witches.

VI.

From north, from south, from east, from west,
As by one kindred aim possest,
Four singing shadows rush together
Towards the old gibbet in the heather;
One passes by the lads and blows
Their sole light vainly as she goes;
The blood within their bodies froze
    At the meeting of the witches.

VII.

Now round the gallows in a ring
They dance, and as they dance, they sing.
But look! for by the saints alive!
They were but four, they now are five;
And 'mid their shadowy garments grey
A taller, blacker form than they
Now crouches down, now leaps away!
    The Devil's with the witches!

·The Witches

The candle-flame burns low and sick,
And wastes upon the slanted wick ;
The lad who holds it 's like to die,
With beating heart and palsied eye ;
One minute more, one minute more,
And the whole country-side 's given o'er
To demons from the night's black shore
    And malice-working witches!

But still his English heart is stout,
And, seeing the flame is well-nigh out,
With purs'd lips, as one plays the flute,
He darts up to the gibbet's root ;
And on the bed that no dew wets
Of moss and whortle-leaves, he sets
His candle-end, and straight forgets
    His fear of ghastly witches.

In time! in time! with scream and start,
The black descends, the grey depart ;
A sulphurous smell invades the brain,

The Witches

But passes in a whiff of rain.
The morning straight begins to break ;
The cocks in Canvil farmstead wake ;
The numb world breathes, all for the sake
  Of midnight-harrying witches.

XI.

Now back to town the yokels pass ;
Sweet dew falls fresh upon the grass ;
From elms within the coppice-pale
Shouts nightingale to nightingale ;
The web of stars fades out of sight,
In heavenly odour sinks the night,
The spell is gone, the air is light,
    Set free from weight of witches.

XII.

Nor will they come again this year,
To blast our harvest in the ear,
Or kill our cattle, or, passing by,
Breathe on our babes and make them die ;
Men who can dare at night to bring
Clear candle-light to the shameful thing,
And set flame down in the ghastly ring,
    Need fear no more from witches.

THE DEATH OF PROCRIS

TO J. E. H.

POOR jealous Procris in the Cretan wood,
   Slain by the very hand of love at last !
This way was best ! the cordial bath of blood,
   The long love-sickness past.

The brown fauns gather round with piteous cries ;
   They mourn her beauty, guess not at her woe ;
They find no Eos graven on those eyes
      Whence tears no longer flow.

Her griefs, her frailties from the flowery turf
   Exhaled, are as the dews of yesterday ;
The grim ship hurrying through the Phocian surf,
   The exile on her way,

The Death of Procris

The cruel goddess, and the two-fold test,
  The breaking heart of hate, the poisoned hours, —
All these have faded into utter rest
      Among the Cretan flowers.

Ah! wrap her body in its fluttering lawns!
  'T is Cephalus' own shaft that hath made cease
The passion of her breast; hush, foolish fauns,
      Hush! for her end was peace.

THE GARDEN OF CHRIST'S

TO W. R. S.

BENEATH this turf lie roses whose pale
    blood
    The very hand of Milton may have shed,
    Or wreck of bays once pleated for the head
Of Quarles, whose early modesty withstood
No well-meant clamour of a student-brood ;
    Great poets here, and Platonists long dead,
    By feathered Clio and Urania led,
Have waited for the moment and the mood.
Ah ! who shall say these warm and russet walls,
This lustrous pool upon whose mirror falls
    The shadow of so many an ancient tree,
Embrace not still the past, as perfumes hold
The spirits of flowers that may no more unfold
    Their living buds by any lake or lea ?

A SYRIAN INSCRIPTION

BENEATH this arch, I, Tabnit, lie at rest,
I, Tabnit, Priest of Ashtoreth, and King
Of Sidon where the tideless waters swing.
O man, with hands and footsteps all unblest,
Who comest, an unseasonable guest,
Depart in haste, nor o'er my ashes fling
Thy furtive shadow.   Go, nor dream I bring
Silver and gold for thy unhallowed quest.

Else, — if this screed thou connest, and dost yet
Presume upon my slumber, —be there shed
The curse of Ashtoreth on thy moon-struck head ;
Thee may the living in thy life forget,
No seed in fields of childhood mayest thou set,
Nor couch at last among the peaceful dead.

THE PICTURE OF VIRTUE

Imitated from the Latin of Théodore de Beza

W HAT form art thou in rags?
      Child of the most pure skies.
Why is thy robe so vile?
      Vain riches I despise.
And why this double face?
      To note ill fate and good.
What doth this bridle teach?
      That rage must be subdued.
This mattock in thy hand?
      Labour is dear to me.
And wings to win the stars?
      And higher, if higher may be.
These bands across thy breast?
      That in the grave I lie.
These feet that tread down Death?
      I, only, cannot die.

THE MARRIED BIBLIOPHIL

After the Swedish of C. D. af Wirsén

STILL dumb thou sittest, with a downcast
   look,
The world forgetting o'er a brown old book;

While she who ever would embrace thee tries
In silence to caress thee with her eyes.

Say not so sharply, " Leave me here in peace!"
Nay! leave thy book, and from dull reading cease;

Since many a man who sits alone, perplexed,
Would yield all else so to be teased and vexed.

Give up thy book of life for love to paint
With golden pictures of a household saint,

The Married Bibliophil

With miniatures whose blazon may provide
For days that shall grow dark, a light and guide;

So when thou turn'st the page where Love struck
  blind
Thy bookish eyes, an angel thou shalt find.

TO A BIBLIOMANIAC

Paraphrased from an Epigram of Ausonius

BECAUSE your books are richly bound,
    You feel a scholar through and through?
Then one Cremona, smooth and sound,
    Would make a fiddler of you too!

Emptis quod libris tibi bibliotheca referta est,
    Doctum et grammaticum te, Philomuse, putas?
Hoc genere et chordas, et plectra, et barbita conde;
    Omnia mercatus, cras citharoedus eris!

Aus., *Epig.* xliv.

THE SICK GARDENER

BRING no valerian from the wall
  That once I climbed in June,
Nor dropping pinks, nor larkspurs tall,
  Nor pansies like the moon, —
Great nodding pansies, grave and pale
With listening to the night-wind's tale;

Nor whitest Canterbury bells,
  Nor sturdy-hearted stocks,
Moth-like petunias, musk that smells
  Like Love among the rocks,
Geraniums lilac, pink and red,
Nor thyme that's sweet when time is dead;

But in those garden-walks where I
  Was young so long ago,
Howe'er the bees may chaffer, buy
  One bunch of elder-snow;

The Sick Gardener

Its vapid white and sickly green
Remind me best of what has been.

Ambition foiled by lack of power,
   Youth that burned out too soon,
A pulse that falters hour by hour,
   Blithe chords struck out of tune, —
All this the Elder Blossom says
At sunset of my weary days.

RUIN

AS I was walking in my lunar dream
Up those dim stairs that lead to break of day,
My soul's Chimera barred the starry way,
And broke the thread-like hope, the glimmering
beam;

Methought my spirit pealed a stifled scream, —
So hideous-fair the monster, loud and gay,
So turbulent and blithe, in riotous play.
It called upon me, shouting, to blaspheme:

And my weak flesh, pledg'd to God's work and
word,
Discreet and mild, subdued to yearn and learn,
Almost redeemed, a blanching miracle, —
Flushing deep red, with acrid juices stirred,
Before this vast brute, gross and taciturn,
Rolled, crashing, back into the heart of hell.

OPIUM HARVEST

HIGH up in hollow valleys where dim lakes
   In Karahissar find no water-shed,
   By many a swarthy snow-gorged river-bed,
In long white fluttering waves the poppy shakes ;

But spring-tide comes 'at last, and April wakes,
   And tears the petals from the golden head,
   Till, of its pink wings disinherited,
The opium-laden capsule bends and bakes.

Then, after sunset, the sleek farmers creep
   To slash the poppy-globes, and leave them soon
   Oozing green tears beneath the gibbous moon ;

Tears, that in scallop-shells, when dawn shall peep,
   Patient, they 'll gather ; then, dismiss the boon
Round the wide world in bales of solid sleep.

Exotic Sonnets

GUSTAF ROSENHANE

(1619–1684)

I.

D EEP in a vale where rocks on every side
Shut out the winds, and scarcely let the sun
Between them dart his rays down one by one,
Where all was still and cool in summer-tide,
And softly, with her whispering waves that sighed,
A little river, that had scarce begun
Her silver course, made bold to fleet and run
Down leafy falls to woodlands dense and wide,
There slept a tiny plain just large enow
To give small mountain-folk right room to dance,
With oaks and limes and maples ringed around;
Hither I came, and viewed its turf askance,
Its solitude with beauty seemed a-glow, —
My Love had walked there and 't was holy ground!

A ND then I sat me down, and gave the rein
   To my wild thoughts, till many a song
      that rang
From leafy boughs where hidden warblers sang
Recalled me from myself; then " Ah ! in vain,"
I said, " do these outpour the tender strain ?
   Can these sweet birds that with such airs harangue
   Their feathered loves, like me, feel sorrow's pang ?
Ah ! would that I, like them, had pinions twain !
Straight would I fly to her whom I love best,
   Nor vainly warbling in the woodland sing,
But chirp my prayer, and preen my plumèd crest,
   And to this spot once more her beauty bring,
   And flutter round her flight with supple wing,
And lead her to my secret leafy nest."

OLOF WEXIONIUS

(1656–1690)

ON THE DEATH OF A PIOUS LADY

THE earthly roses at God's call have made
    Way, lady, for a dress of heavenly white,
In which thou walk'st with other figures bright,
Once loved on earth, who now, like thee arrayed,
Feast on two-fold ambrosia, wine and bread ;
    They lead thee up by sinuous paths of light
    Through lilied fields that sparkle in God's sight,
And crown thee with delights that never fade.
O thou thrice-sainted mother, in that bliss,
Forget not thy two daughters, whom a kiss
    At parting left as sad as thou art glad ;
In thy deep joy think how for thee they weep,
Or conjure through the shifting glass of sleep,
    The saint heaven hath, the mother they once had.

ERIK JOHAN STAGNELIUS

(1793–1823)

I.

HOPE REPULSED

U P through the ruins of my earthly dreams
I catch the stars of immortality ;
What store of joy can hide in heaven for me ?
What further hope feed those celestial gleams ?
Can there be other grapes whose nectar streams
  For me, whom earth's vine fails ? oh ! can it be
  That this abandoned heart again may see
A forehead garlanded, an eye that beams ?
Alas ! 't is childhood's dream that vanisheth !
  The heaven-born soul that feigns it can return,
  And end in peace this hopeless strife with fate !
There is no backward step ; 't is only death
  Can quench at last these wasting fires that burn,
  Can break the chain, the captive liberate.

MEMORY

O CAMP of flowers, with poplars girdled round,
　　Grey guardians of life's soft and purple bud !
O silver spring, beside whose brimming flood
My pensive childhood, its Elysium found !
O happy hours by love and fancy crowned,
　　Whose horn of plenty flatteringly subdued
　　My heart into a trance, whence, with a rude
And horrid blast, fate came my soul to hound !
Who was the goddess that empowered you all
　　Thus to bewitch me ?　Out of wasting snow
　　And lily-leaves her head-dress should be made !
Weep, my poor lute ! nor on Astræa call,
　　She will not smile, nor I, who mourn below,
　　Till I, a shade in heaven, clasp her, a shade.

LUNA

DEEP slumber hung o'er sea and hill and
plain ;
With pale pink cheek fresh from her watery caves
Slow rose the moon out of the midnight waves,
Like Venus out of ocean born again ;
Then blazed Olympian on the dark blue main ;
" So shall, my star," hark how my weak hope
raves !
" My happy star ascend the sea that laves
Its shores with grief, and silence all my pain ! "
With that there sighed a wandering midnight
breeze,
High up among the topmost tufted trees,
And o'er the moon's face blew a veil of cloud ;

Luna

And in the breeze my genius spake, and said,
" While thy heart stirs, thy glimmering hope has
fled,
And like the moon lies muffled in a shroud."

PIETER CORNELISZOON HOOFT

I.

TO HUGO GROTIUS

GREAT soul, that with the keenness of clear
sight
Just measure takest of approaching things,
 Yet by the wisdom that high memory brings
Dost hold full judgment of all past years' flight,
What God or man in counsel or of right
 May speak, thou can'st expound ; from thee light
 springs ;
 Thou art the eye of Holland ; when storm rings
In starless weather, thou dost lift thy light.
Sun of our sphere, how shall I liken you ?

To Hugo Grotius

Art thou a blast that God from heaven out-blew,
  Come to our hearts, to find them well prepared ?
Or, from the roofs of paradise, a spirit,
Dowered with all skill that sons of light inherit,
  Whose wit and power our earth with heaven hath
    shared ?

Sept. 3, 1616

FRIENDSHIP

THIS earth, embossed with mountains, laced
    with streams,
Starred with fair cities ringed about with towers,
Whose face with hill and laughing valley gleams,
    Whose shadowy woods are full of tender flowers,
The birds, the careless beasts beneath the moon,
    And that conceited race of feeble man,
All hold their place by harmony, and soon
    Sans friendship would sink out of nature's plan.
From manly friendship cities take their root,
    Their nurture and their life ; from strife their
        death ;
    Thro' civil jars they pant with heavy breath ;
        So dangerous is division in the State !
In harmony the seeds of glory shoot,
    And peace at home makes little kingdoms great.

JOOST VAN VONDEL

ON THE TRUCE OF THE NETHERLANDS

1609

H EAVEN, tired of war, takes pity on our
woes;
Castille herself is moved to grant us rest;
The States give ear; and lo! at their request
The mild peace-makers part us from our foes;
To all delay there comes at length a close.
For two brief years, or three, at Heaven's behest,
They offer truce, and Holland thus possess'd
Of hope at last, sighs, glad of her repose.
Nassau disarms himself, and, wearily,

Joost Van Vondel

Puts up his sword, notched in so many a fight,
And our United Land in her delight
Sends up to God her altar-fires of praise.
    Now to the Lord of Hosts our thanks we cry
Who gives us gladness after many days.

CERVANTES

WHEN I was marked for suffering, Love
forswore
All knowledge of my doom ; or else at ease
Love grows a cruel tyrant, hard to please ;
Or else a chastisement exceeding sore
A little sin hath brought me. Hush ! no more !
Love is a god ! all things he knows and sees,
And gods are bland and mild ! Who then decrees
The dreadful woe I bear and yet adore ?
If I should say, O Chloë, that 't was thou
I should speak falsely, since, being wholly good
Like Heaven itself, from thee no ill may come.
There is no hope ; I must die shortly now,
Not knowing why, since sure no witch hath
brewed
The drug that might avert my martyrdom.

The Masque of Painters:

AS PERFORMED BY THE ROYAL INSTITUTE
OF PAINTERS IN WATER COLOURS, ON
MAY 19, 1885, AND SUCCESSIVE
NIGHTS

THE MASQUE OF PAINTERS

So soon as the PRINCE *and* PRINCESS *of* WALES
*were seated, there was heard music from the Guards'
Band. This being ended with a flourish of trumpets
and drums, there was discovered an altar, beside which*
VIRGIL *stood, attired in a long robe of scarlet, with a
crown of laurel upon his head, and a staff in his hand.
He spoke as follows : —*

FROM my Italian grave I rise to-night,
    Once more to move on earth in live men's
        sight ;
The blare of trumpets, music's festal sound,
Disturbed my sacred slumbers underground ;
So once I rose, upon the wild hill-side,
When Dante saw the three fierce beasts, and cried ;
So hand in hand with him I walked to tell
Of Paradise, of Purgatory, and Hell.

The Masque of Painters

Know 't is Athene's will this night that we
Should witness here a matchless pageantry ;
Your eyes, unsealed, shall view as much as mine,
And glory in a fabulous design ;
Keep silence then, while I declare aloud
What gorgeous pomp shall break from yonder cloud,
What summons brings the gay procession by,
And whence to-night it hither comes, and why.

Ye have heard of old, in proverb and in song,
How that though life be brief, yet art is long ;
Upon this stage to-night before we part
Ye shall behold the pedigree of art ;
And find for once, beneath my magic rhyme, —
For once concentr'd in one hour of time, —
All that since Art's first dewy days hath sped
By various modes in divers fashions led.

Nor shall the Painters only grace your sight,
The Kings they wrought for shall be seen
        to-night ;
The Soldiers, too, who served adventure far,
And clashed their armour in the storm of war ;

The Masque of Painters

The Poets mild, with laurel round their hair,
And stately Dames imperishably fair,
The scarlet Trumpeter, the snow-white Saint, —
All that the painter's hand delights to paint.

Now first behold, soon as the hautboys cease,
Come shadowy names from fair historic Greece:
Phidias, whose men like marble mountains shone,
And he who reared the stately Parthenon,
Zeuxis, on whom the birds of heaven attend,
With wise *Apelles*, Alexander's friend ;
And midst them all, the mighty statesman moves
Who ruled amid the embowering olive-groves.

*The curtain fell, and loud music sounded as
before. The inner scene then opened, and revealed
part of a street in Athens. On the right hand
scaffolding discovered against a building. Among loose
blocks of marble in the foreground* PERICLES *consult-
ing* ICTINUS *the architect and* PHIDIAS *the sculptor
respecting the details of the Parthenon.* ZEUXIS
*was seen on the left hand, in converse with some
Athenian ladies.*

The Masque of Painters

The scene presently closed, and, after orchestral music as before, the band summoned VIRGIL *with a flourish of trumpets, and the scene opening, discovered him ready to speak : —*

Ages have passed, and lo! before me stand
The new-born glories of the Tuscan land :
Dante, with whom I trode the shores of hell ;
And *Beatrice,* whom he loved so well ;
Giotto, whom wandering *Cimabue* found,
A mountain-shepherd, scrawling on the ground ;
And all whom young Italian spring-tide filled
With godlike rage to paint or carve or build.

No names so great as these the ages know —
Da Vinci, Raphael, Michelangelo ;
All skill, all grace, all power of hand and heart,
These mighty three combined t' enrich their art ;
And till the tired world sinks within the sea,
No fourth shall rise to breast the immortal three.

The Adriatic raised her salt-strewn head,
And saw her Venice glow with rosy red ;
Not sunset then, nor sunrise, but the brush
Of *Giorgione* spread this ruddy flush ;

The Masque of Painters

There *Titian's* noon-day flamed, there the moon set
In *Veronese*, and night in *Tintoret*.

*After the curtain had fallen, amid music, the inner
scene opened again, and was shown divided into three
arched compartments, designed to display, as in a
triptych, the arts of Florence, Rome, and Venice.
In the centre, in a Florentine garden full of cypresses
and orange-trees, behind which rose the tower of the
Palazzo Vecchio,* DANTE *appeared with* BEATRICE,
PETRARCH *with* LAURA, CIMABUE *with* GIOTTO, *as a
shepherd boy, also* NICCOLÒ PISANO, *an angel with
a zither, and certain ladies of Florence, among whom*
BOCCACCIO'S FIAMETTA *was discovered.*

*On the right hand, the scene displayed a terrace
in the gardens of the Vatican.* MICHELANGELO,
standing on the steps, was showing to Pope JULIUS II.
*an architectural design. Cardinal and priests were
in waiting on his Holiness.* RAPHAEL *at the foot
of the steps in front gazed upon his great rival.*

*On the left was seen a glimpse of Venice from a
balcony of the Ducal Palace looking on the Grand
Canal with the column of S. Mark, and the island of
San Georgio beyond. A gentleman of the Giorgione*

The Masque of Painters

period, in the costume of a companion of the Calza, with a mandolin in his hand, sat, looking up at two Venetian ladies nobly habited. A Venetian Senator, an Oriental Ambassador, and GIOVANNI BELLINI *were also seen in the balcony, while from the front* TITIAN *and* PAUL VERONESE *contemplated the group.*

The scene then closed, and the band once more summoned VIRGIL *with a flourish of trumpets. The curtains opening, he spoke as follows : —*

Plain burghers these, who claimed response from art
To simple instincts of a northern heart,
Dürer, the prince of German handicraft,
And stalwart *Visscher*, and brave *Adam Kraft*,
Cranach, the friend of Luther, poet *Sachs*,
All sturdy subjects of grim Kaiser *Max*.

Till *Holbein* came to paint in stately scenes
Our own bluff Henry's court, and half his queens,
No art appeared, in this chill land of ours,
To strew the barren road of life with flowers;
Erasmus, More, Melancthon, these we see,
Great friends of his, — yet none so great as he.

152

The Masque of Painters

The tableau displayed the interior of a studio in which ALBRECHT DÜRER *was explaining to the Emperor* MAXIMILIAN *his print called the " Triumph " of that potentate. In the group supporting the Emperor were* HOLBEIN, PETER VISSCHER, *and* LUCAS CRANACH.

The scene closed, and, after music, the curtain again parted and revealed VIRGIL, *who spoke as follows :*—

From Flemish guilds in towns on dune and dyke
Come forth the fur-robed forms of each *Van Eyck ;*
There *Van der Weyden* walks; there grave and staid
Tall *Memlinck* bends above the shrine he made,
While sparkling, jewel-like and dewy-bright,
Their clean enamelled paintings bask in light.

The Dutch, when wealth and wisdom clipped their
    wings,
First learned the loveliness of homely things ;
But looked beyond, for *Rembrandt* trained their eyes,
And marked the changes of their northern skies ;
Then silvery *Terburg* came, and golden *Cuyp,*
And each flushed votary of the pot and pipe.

The Masque of Painters

The curtain fell, and, after music, the scene rose and displayed an old Dutch house and garden in Haarlem, once the home of FRANZ HALS *and of* JAN VAN DER MEER. *On the right were a group drinking and talking around a table,* REMBRANDT *lifting his glass to* CUYP; OSTADE *and* TENIERS *watching a game of bowls.*

The scene closed, and, after a flourish of trumpets, VIRGIL *appeared once more, and spoke as follows: —*

To that pale court where passion burned in flame,
With silver gifts and bronze, *Cellini* came;
There chained to pleasure, art and beauty lay,
And all the Pleiad with their crowns of bay;
At Francis' feet the mighty Potter laid
The coloured fish and snakes and weeds he made,
And round them wondering those French faces drew
That *Clouet's* brush and *Goujon's* chisel knew.

The scene represented a terrace in front of the palace of Fontainebleau; FRANCIS I. *receiving* BEN-VENUTO CELLINI, *who was taking specimens of gold and silver plate from his pupils* PAOLO ROMANO *and*

The Masque of Painters

ASCANIO DA TAGLIACOZZO, *and presenting them to the King.*

VIRGIL *appeared again, as the scene closed, and spoke as follows : —*

The Spanish Don, pragmatical and proud,
Disdained the simple arts that please the crowd ;
Murillo's gay Madonnas charmed the court,
But painting's days in Spain were starv'd and short ;
Yet long enough to add *Velasquez'* name
To that brief deathless roll of finished fame.

The scene represented the studio of VELASQUEZ, *in Madrid, on the occasion of a royal visit. The Master was pointing out to King* PHILIP IV. *and his Queen his picture of "Las Meniñas," which stood upon an easel.* ALONZO CANO *was standing behind the painter, and Cardinal* GASPAR DE BORJA, *in company with Doña* MARCELLA DE ULLOA, *behind the Queen. The King, leaning on the arm of Cardinal* ROSPIGLIOSI, *was in the act of decorating* VELASQUEZ *with the order of the cross of Santiago.*

At the close of the scene, VIRGIL *being again summoned by the drums and trumpets, spoke thus : —*

The Masque of Painters

Prince of the world of painters, *Rubens* comes
And storms it with his trumpets and his drums;
Then on our aching ears less rudely strike
The courtlier accents of the grave *Vandyke,*
Whose brush the secret from a *Charles* could wring
How sorrow sits on eyelids of a king.

Now, in the days when German Georges ruled
And bullying Fritz his stiff-backed squadron schooled,
Hogarth appears, — in whom the graver's gift
Ranks with the pen of Fielding and of Swift,
Since, like the Beadle of the Morals, he
Lashed through the streets the cur Hypocrisy.

And here, at last, the English painters come,
Sir Joshua's glowing palette on his thumb,
Angelica, unfortunate and fair,
And *Gainsborough* with his liberal wealth of air;
George Morland, Wilson, Romney, close the race,
The last of Englishmen to dress with grace.

*The tableau represented a hemicycle in a pyramidal
shape, rising between columns. At the summit stood
CHARLES I. in hunting costume, and Queen HENRI-
ETTA MARIA, in conversation with RUBENS; just*

The Masque of Painters

below them stood VANDYKE, *painting a portrait of the King, and on successive steps, broadening to the base, were* HOGARTH, *standing a little aloof from the others, Sir* JOSHUA REYNOLDS *conversing with* ANGELICA KAUFFMANN, *and* GAINSBOROUGH.

The scene closed, and VIRGIL, *appearing for the last time, addressed the company as follows :* —

PRINCE and PRINCESS, the show is done, and these
Once more retire across your narrow seas,
Since few of all this glorious train were bred
With the English leopards flying o'er their head ;

Yet have we too an art that England claims,
Nor this unwedded to illustrious names ;
Fresco and oils we learned from over sea
But no one drew in aqua-tint till we ;
And, now in all lands, cunning artists use
To paint in English wise, in watery hues.

These who have passed before your eyes to-night
Pursue this art, transparent, graceful, light,
Content to move along the humbler road,
And bend their painting to this native mode,

The Masque of Painters

Proud to remember *Girtin's* ruined scene,
The tender wash of *Cozens'* silver-green,
Glover's soft touch, *Paul Sandby* cold and stern,
The trees of *Edridge* and the streams of *Hearne*,
Turner whose wondrous art summed up the rest, —
Great Nature's boldest pupil and her best, —
The new Prometheus, who from Heaven has won,
Not fire, but light, but splendour of the sun ;
And with him all who since his day have striven
To paint our world beneath the arch of heaven.

Then, ere I vanish, ah ! let *Virgil* plead
For this home growth of art, this British weed :
And still among your foreign flowers find room
Close to your hearts for one wild English bloom.

*With which the whole ended, and the company
began to dance.*

PRINTED BY JOHN WILSON AND SON
AT THE UNIVERSITY PRESS IN CAM-
BRIDGE FOR STONE AND KIMBALL,
PUBLISHERS, OF CHICAGO.
OCTOBER : MDCCCXCIV.